Dear Parent:
Your child's love of reading starts here!

Every child learns to read in a different way and at his or her own speed. Some go back and forth between reading levels and read favorite books again and again. Others read through each level in order. You can help your young reader improve and become more confident by encouraging his or her own interests and abilities. From books your child reads with you to the first books he or she reads alone, there are I Can Read Books for every stage of reading:

SHARED READING
Basic language, word repetition, and whimsical illustrations, ideal for sharing with your emergent reader

BEGINNING READING
Short sentences, familiar words, and simple concepts for children eager to read on their own

READING WITH HELP
Engaging stories, longer sentences, and language play for developing readers

READING ALONE
Complex plots, challenging vocabulary, and high-interest topics for the independent reader

ADVANCED READING
Short paragraphs, chapters, and exciting themes for the perfect bridge to chapter books

I Can Read Books have introduced children to the joy of reading since 1957. Featuring award-winning authors and illustrators and a fabulous cast of beloved characters, I Can Read Books set the standard for beginning readers.

A lifetime of discovery begins with the magical words **"I Can Read!"**

Visit www.icanread.com for information
on enriching your child's reading experience.

For my C-O-U-S-I-N-S
Penny and Johnny
—J.O'C.

For my nephew William, who
is splendid at lots of things!
—R.P.G.

For Igraine, an excellent
woman of letters.
Twenty-six, to be precise.
—T.E.

I Can Read Book® is a trademark of HarperCollins Publishers.

Library of Congress Cataloging-in-Publication Data is available.
ISBN 978-0-06-200176-4 (trade bdg.) — ISBN 978-0-06-200175-7 (pbk.)

15 16 17 18 19 20 SCP 10 9 8 7 6 5 4
❖
First Edition

Fancy NANCY

Splendid Speller

by Jane O'Connor

cover illustration by Robin Preiss Glasser

interior illustrations by Ted Enik

HARPER

An Imprint of HarperCollinsPublishers

I don't mean to brag,

but I am a splendid speller.

S-P-L-E-N-D-I-D.

(Splendid is even better than great.)

Bree is a splendid speller too.

We practice spelling

in our clubhouse after school.

I can even spell in French!

C-H-I-E-N means "dog."

You say it like this—SHEE-enn.

My sister is very impressed.

(Impressed means

she thinks I'm great.)

My sister cannot spell any words.

My parents spell out stuff

they don't want her to hear.

They used to fool me this way,

but not anymore.

She has to get a shot,

S-H-O-T,

at her checkup tomorrow.

At school today, Ms. Glass says,

"Our first spelling test

is on Friday."

Here is the list of test words.

pass   glass

class   happy

sad   glad

mad   peek

week   giggle

We write down the words.

Some kids make faces.

They think the words are hard.

But Bree and I are happy.

H-A-P-P-Y.

This test will be easy!

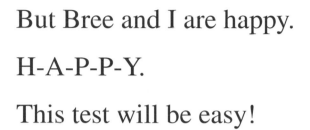

At dinner I practice some words.

"Please P-A-S-S the carrots.

May I have a G-L-A-S-S of milk?"

Dad claps and says, "Bravo!"

"I don't mean to brag," I say,

"but Bree and I

are the best spellers

in the C-L-A-S-S."

Later I memorize

the harder words.

(Memorize is fancy for

learn by heart.)

The hardest is "giggle."

G-I-G-G-L-E.

It has so many Gs!

I practice all week.

W-E-E-K.

It will be splendid

to spell every word right.

By Friday I am ready.

Ms. Glass says each word slowly.

The last one is "giggle."

I write down G-I-G-L-E.

Is that right?

I am not sure.

I try it another way.

G-I-G-G-L-E.

Is that right?

Then I do something wicked.

(Wicked is way worse than bad.)

I peek, P-E-E-K, at Bree's paper!

Bree has G-I-G-G-L-E.

I bet Bree is right.

I start to fix my word.

I want to get all the words right.

I want to be a splendid speller.

Then I stop.

"No, no, no," I say to myself.

I hand in my test to Ms. Glass.

If she knew I peeked,

I bet she would hate me!

At the playground,

I do not play with any kids.

At lunch,

I do not eat my cookies.

I do not sing in music.

At the end of the day,

we get back our tests.

I got one wrong.

"Giggle."

Miss Glass takes me aside.

"What's wrong, Nancy?" she asks.

"Are you upset about the test?

You did very well."

I tell her what I did.

I cry so hard I get hiccups.

"I am a wicked cheater."

Ms. Glass says,

"Nancy, it was wrong

to peek at Bree's paper.

But you did not cheat.

You stopped before you cheated.

I am proud of you for that."

"You are?" I say.

I still feel sad.

S-A-D.

But I do not feel so wicked.

On the way home,

I confess to Bree.

(Confess means telling

something bad you did.)

She forgives me.

Fancy Nancy's Fancy Words

These are the fancy words in this book:

Chien—"dog" in French (you say it like this: SHEE-enn)

Confess—telling someone something bad that you did

Impressed—thinking someone or something is great

Memorize—learn by heart

Splendid—even better than great

Wicked—way worse than bad

She shows me her test.

"I forgot a *p* in 'happy,'" she says.

Maybe we are not always

splendid spellers,

but we are always splendid friends!

"I just needed a little love."
I say, "Me, too, Grandma!"

I say, "Grandma, I thought you weren't feeling well."
Grandma says, "I wasn't.

Here we are.

Grandma is not in bed.

She is sitting with Grandpa.

Dad starts the car.

We have a nice slow drive

all the rest of the way.

Dad does not look too happy.

We all give Dad some love.

Now he will feel better.

He is a state trooper.

He gives Dad a ticket,

but not for a ball game.

A man on a motorcycle
with flashing lights
tells Dad to pull over.

The water pours everywhere.
I say thank you and leave.

I need to use the bathroom.

Dad stops at a gas station.

I flush the toilet.

Dad picks up the turtle.

Dad puts him in the grass.

He is safe. We wave good-bye.

I see a turtle in the road.
"Dad!" I say. "Save the turtle.
Turtles need love, too."

It is time to leave.

I say good-bye to my pets.

They look sad. I hug them.

We have no egg salad.

Mom is sad.

She needs a little love.

Kitty finds the egg salad.
Oh, no! Blue finds it, too!

Little Sister says,
"My other dolls are lonely.
They need lots of love."

18

Little Sister brings her dolls
to show Grandma.
Mom says, "No, take two."

Blue says, "Yelp!"

Now Blue needs a little love.

Blue feels better.

I carry the apples to the car.

I do not see Blue.

I step on Blue's tail.

I do not cry much.

Dad gives me some love.

I feel better.

We pick apples for Grandma.

We put them in a basket.

I fall off the ladder.

But a bee stings her.
Mom gives her a little love.
Then she feels better.

Little Sister picks flowers
just for Grandma.

"Look, Mom," I say.
"Blue loves olives, too!"

Mom makes egg salad.

She puts olives in it.

I love olives, but I spill them.

I draw a get well card
just for Grandma.
Little Sister helps.

We decide to go and
cheer her up with love.

Grandpa calls and says
Grandma isn't feeling very well.

For the children, teachers, and families of Sandy Hook,
with all my love.

I Can Read Book® is a trademark of HarperCollins Publishers.

Little Critter: Just a Little Love

Library of Congress card number: 2013938122
ISBN 978-0-06-207196-5 (trade bdg.)—ISBN 978-0-06-147815-4 (pbk.)
13   14   15   16   17   LP/WOR   10   9   8   7   6   5   4   3   2   1
❖
First Edition

A Big Tuna Trading Company, LLC/J.R. Sansevere Book
www.littlecritter.com

JUST A
LITTLE LOVE

BY MERCER MAYER

HARPER

An Imprint of HarperCollinsPublishers

Dear Parent:
Your child's love of reading starts here!

Every child learns to read in a different way and at his or her own speed. Some go back and forth between reading levels and read favorite books again and again. Others read through each level in order. You can help your young reader improve and become more confident by encouraging his or her own interests and abilities. From books your child reads with you to the first books he or she reads alone, there are I Can Read Books for every stage of reading:

SHARED READING
Basic language, word repetition, and whimsical illustrations, ideal for sharing with your emergent reader

BEGINNING READING
Short sentences, familiar words, and simple concepts for children eager to read on their own

READING WITH HELP
Engaging stories, longer sentences, and language play for developing readers

READING ALONE
Complex plots, challenging vocabulary, and high-interest topics for the independent reader

ADVANCED READING
Short paragraphs, chapters, and exciting themes for the perfect bridge to chapter books

I Can Read Books have introduced children to the joy of reading since 1957. Featuring award-winning authors and illustrators and a fabulous cast of beloved characters, I Can Read Books set the standard for beginning readers.

A lifetime of discovery begins with the magical words **"I Can Read!"**

Visit www.icanread.com for information
on enriching your child's reading experience.